THE FABULOUS FOSKETT FAMILY CIRCUS

Quentin Blake & John Yeoman

ANDERSEN PRESS

Roll up, roll up, the Foskett Family's
Here to offer lots of fun:
Circus acts to thrill you all,
From five years old to ninety-one.

When Min and Fred put up the flags
It raises lots of smiles –
They pull them out of young Tom's hat,
For miles and miles and miles.

Honk, honk! It's Uncle Decimus performing on his scooter.
His parrot hopes that one day, too, he'll have a little hooter.

Philbert's tops at juggling eggs, he keeps them in the air;
No matter if he drops a few – he's got a lot to spare.

Aunt Esmerelda Foskett does a most amazing thing –
She makes the dog and birds do tricks, and then gets them to sing.

There's no one as gay as our plump Auntie May
With her wonderful hairstyle and floral display.

The tricks that Jess and Bess perform you really can't believe –
You can be sure that every time they've something up their sleeve.

While Rufus holds the hoop in place
Young Dorkin gives the bone a shake.
I think the look on Towser's face
Says "Couldn't you afford a steak?"

Millicent and Flossie and their parrot (named Jerome)
Make balancing look easy –
But don't try this at home!

See the famous Foskett Trio, watch them staggering around;
Marvel that they do all this at least six inches off the ground.

When Alfie's performing with Nathan and Claire
He does it with skill and in style –
He flips a back somersault high in the air
And gives us a wave and a smile.

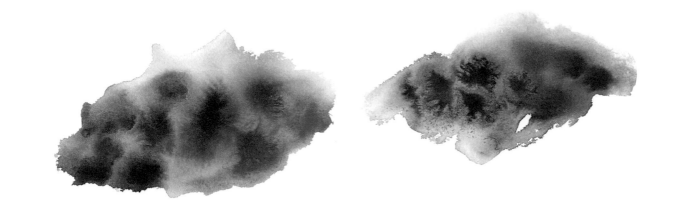

Of all the famous Fosketts there is one you must admire,
That's Uncle Phoenix Foskett, with his daring way with fire.
But Fido's always worried, and prepares himself for flight,
Remembering when the fool breathed in and set his beard alight.

Tansy and Pansy, while having a chat,
Have made a cat's cradle (which won't hold a cat).

Bert and Betsy Foskett are strong in hand and wrist.
There isn't any piece of iron that these two couldn't twist.

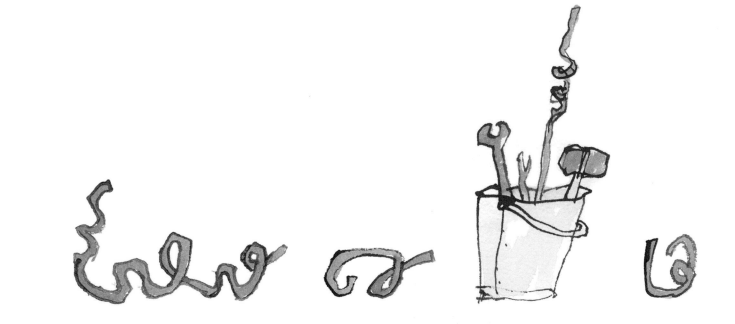

So that's the Foskett Family Circus –
All of them have done their best,
Singing, riding, juggling, tumbling.

Time for them to have a rest.

This paperback first published in 2015 by Andersen Press Ltd.
First published in Great Britain in 2013 by Andersen Press Ltd., 20 Vauxhall Bridge Road, London SW1V 2SA.
Published in Australia by Random House Australia Pty., Level 3, 100 Pacific Highway, North Sydney, NSW 2060.
Text copyright © John Yeoman, 2013. Illustration copyright © Quentin Blake, 2013.
The rights of John Yeoman and Quentin Blake to be identified as the author and illustrator
of this work have been asserted by them in accordance with the Copyright, Designs and Patents Act, 1988.
All rights reserved. Colour separated in Switzerland by Photolitho AG, Zürich.
Printed in China.

10   9   8   7   6   5   4   3   2   1

British Library Cataloguing in Publication Data available.

Trade ISBN 978 1 78344 035 1
Special Sales ISBN 978 1 78344 251 5